Sunrise, Sunset

LYRICS BY **Sheldon Harnick** ∼ MUSIC BY **Jerry Bock**

ILLUSTRATED BY **Ian Schoenherr**

HarperCollinsPublishers

For Charlotte and Sam

Is this the little girl I carried?
Is this the little boy at play?

I don't remember growing older.
When did they?

When did she get to be a beauty?
When did he grow to be so tall?

Wasn't it yesterday

when they were small?

Sunrise, sunset,
Sunrise, sunset,
Swiftly flow the days;

Seedlings turn overnight to sunflow'rs,

Blossoming even as we gaze.

Sunrise, sunset,
Sunrise, sunset,
Swiftly fly the years;

One season following another,

Laden with happiness and tears.

Now is the little boy a bridegroom,
Now is the little girl a bride.

Under the canopy I see them,
Side by side.

Place the gold ring around her finger,
Share the sweet wine and break the glass;
Soon the full circle will have come to pass.

Sunrise, sunset,
   Sunrise, sunset,
      Swiftly flow the days;

Seedlings turn overnight to sunflow'rs,
Blossoming even as we gaze.

Sunrise, Sunset

LYRICS BY **Sheldon Harnick** ~ MUSIC BY **Jerry Bock**

Moderately Slow Waltz tempo (soulful and wistful)

Is this the lit-tle girl I car - ried? Is this the lit-tle boy at
Now is the lit-tle boy a bride - groom, Now is the lit-tle girl a

play? I don't re - mem - ber grow - ing old - er. When
bride. Un - der the can - o - py I see them, Side

did they?____ When did she get to be a beau - ty?
by side.____ Place the gold ring a - round her fin - ger,

When did he grow to be so tall? Was - n't it
Share the sweet wine and break the glass; Soon the full

yes - ter - day when they were small?____
cir - cle will have come to pass.____

Sunrise, Sunset • Text and music © 1964, renewed 1992, by Mayerling Productions Ltd. and Jerry Bock Enterprises •
Illustrations copyright © 2005 by Ian Schoenherr • Manufactured in China. • All rights reserved. • www.harperchildrens.com

Library of Congress Cataloging-in-Publication Data Harnick, Sheldon. Sunrise, sunset / lyrics by Sheldon Harnick ;
music by Jerry Bock ; illustrated by Ian Schoenherr. — 1st ed.   p.   cm.   Summary: An illustrated version of the
well-known song about the passage of time, from the musical "Fiddler on the Roof."   ISBN 0-06-051525-2 — ISBN
0-06-051527-9 (lib. bdg.)   1. Children's songs, English—United States—Texts. [1. Songs.] I. Bock, Jerry. II. Schoenherr,
Ian, ill. III. Title. PZ8.3.H2183Su 2005   2004019104   782.42—dc22   CIP   [E]   AC
Typography by Martha Rago   1 2 3 4 5 6 7 8 9 10   ❖   First Edition

The illustrations for this book were made with colored pencil, permanent ink, and acrylic paint on Bristol board.